It's five years since Ben Tennyson last transformed into aliens and fought crime with his cousin Gwen and their Grandpa Max.

Now 15 years old, Ben is once again forced to turn to the Omnitrix to help fight a new and more sinister threat – the HighBreed, DNAliens and the Forever Knights, who team up to take over the world.

The watch-like Omnitrix has re-programmed itself and has a complete set of ten, brand new alien choices for Ben to get to grips with. Helped by his cousin Gwen with her magical powers and Ben's former enemy, Kevin E. Levin, Ben is soon all set to go hero once again!

NOW READ ON . . .

EGMONT
We bring stories to life

This edition first published in Great Britain 2010
by Egmont UK Limited
239 Kensington High Street
London W8 6SA

Adapted by Barry Hutchison

1 3 5 7 9 10 8 6 4 2

Printed and bound in Great Britain

The Forest Stewardship Council (FSC) is an international,
non-governmental organisation dedicated to promoting
responsible management of the world's forests. FSC operates
a system of forest certification and product labelling that
allows consumers to identify wood and wood-based products
from well-managed forests.

For more information about Egmont's paper buying policy,
please visit www.egmont.co.uk/ethicalpublishing
For more information about the FSC, please visit their
website at www.fsc.org

BEN 10 ALIEN FORCE™

PET PROJECT

CHAPTER ONE

SHIP'S SHAPES

In a cavern hidden deep underground, a man named Chadwick was preparing to speak. He was a scientist – a scientist who worked with very dangerous group of people.

'My fellow Knights,' he began, addressing the four armoured Forever Knights who stood before him. The room they were in was Chadwick's lab. Weird alien artefacts covered every surface.

'We have lately endured a grave defeat,' the scientist continued. 'Our prisoner, the villainous Dragon, escaped from our grasp.'

On the screen behind Chadwick, a series of images showed Humungousaur, Kevin and Gwen rescuing a huge, dragon-like creature from another group of Forever Knights. The last photograph showed the dragon's ship blasting off into space.

'But does this mean we have lost?' asked Chadwick. 'Do we now abandon our sacred duty?'

'No!' roared the Forever Knights.

'No. Instead, we must pursue the beast across the void. We must destroy it and its vile species once and for all.'

The knights gave a cheer of approval, their metal gauntlets punching the air.

'And so to that end I have built a star ship, combining dozens of alien technologies we have acquired.'

Across the lab, a series of lights suddenly clicked on, revealing a terrifying-looking spaceship. Every part of the ship was covered in alien weaponry. It had been built for one thing and one thing only: War.

'And though its controls are too complex for human operation, I believe I have found a solution,' continued Chadwick.

The screen behind him changed to show several cars floating in mid-air. A second later it changed to show a woman being pursued by her vacuum cleaner. Finally, it settled on another image. This picture showed a black blob with green markings.

'These recent phenomena are the work of a Galvan Shape-Shifter. Equal parts machine and beast, which can assimilate and duplicate any device it encounters,' Chadwick explained, his eyes blazing with excitement. 'With it, we will create an armada of spacecraft, which we can use to obliterate the Dragon home world!'

A hulking figure stepped from the shadows behind the other knights. He towered above them, his high-tech armour sleeker and far more advanced than theirs.

'I'll catch your little blob from you,' growled the brute, lifting his visor to reveal a battle-scarred face.

'Beware, Sir Morton. It will not be easy to capture.'

A wicked smile crept across Sir Morton's face. 'That's what makes my job all the more interesting, don't it?'

Outside the house of Ben's girlfriend, Julie, something crept quietly through the bushes. It scurried stealthily across the grass, moving quickly towards the back door of the house.

TAP. TAP. TAP.

In the kitchen, Julie was just putting on her jacket. She made for the door, pulled it open, and looked out to find no one there.

She was about to close the door again, when a movement down on the step caught her eye.

Julie smiled as she looked down to find Ship – the shape-shifting alien blob she and Ben had found on their first date – sitting on the step, wagging its stumpy tail.

'Ship, ship, ship, ship, ship!' chattered the blob, excitedly, as Julie followed it out into the garden.

'Where have you been?' asked Julie, kneeling down to give Ship a friendly pat.

'Ship!'

'Yes, hello, I'm glad to see you too,' she laughed. 'OK, Ship, show me a new trick.'

Leaping into the air, Ship's body began to bulge and change. In a flash he transformed into a toaster, popping out slices of black and green toast in all directions.

'That's great!' cried Julie.

Another flash. This time Ship transformed into a full-sized tumble drier.

'Good boy. Good Ship. Anything else?'

Ship didn't need to be asked twice. Leaping into the air he began to change once more. Julie barely had time to leap out of the way before a full-sized nuclear submarine crashed down on to the grass beside her.

'OK, um, change back,' she said, quickly.

Doing as he was told, Ship returned to his normal blob form. Julie looked around at the deep imprint the submarine had left in the grass. Half of the garden fence had also been smashed, and a large tree had been knocked over on to its side.

'How am I supposed to explain that?' she wondered, before the blasting of a nearby car horn caught her attention. 'Oh, gotta go. See you later, OK?'

'Ship. Ship. Ship.'

Julie gave the little blob another pat, then hurried off to where a green car with black stripes was waiting for her.

Opening the back door, Julie slid on to the seat next to Gwen and buckled her seatbelt.

'Are you ready to shop?' asked Gwen, eagerly.

'Gift cards from Grandma,' replied Julie, holding up a stash of gift tokens. 'I am totally ready.'

She and Gwen both squealed with
excitement. In the driver's seat, Kevin winced
and covered his ears.

'OK, no shrieking in the car!' he glowered.

'No promises,' said Gwen. 'Sometimes
we're going to shriek.'

'Yeah, like you and Ben do when you're
watching football,' added Julie.

'We do not shriek!' shrieked Kevin.

He lowered his voice and tried again.

'Uh, shriek.'

'Uh-huh,' laughed Gwen.

'Anyway, I'll drive you to the mall, as promised,' said Kevin, changing the subject, 'but I'm not hanging around and watching you shop.'

'That's OK,' said Gwen with a shrug. 'You're not invited.'

Outside, Ship watched the car begin to pull away. Determined to stay close to Julie, he began hopping after the vehicle, bouncing along faster and faster until he was right behind it.

With a final lunge, Ship hurled himself at the back of the car. His body seemed to turn into liquid as it hit the metal, before being completely absorbed into the paintwork.

The little alien blob felt very pleased with itself. Wherever Julie was going, Ship was going too!

Inside the car, Julie was talking about her favourite subject: Ben!

'And then Ben sent me an IM and said he kinda missed me, too.'

'That is so sweet,' Gwen gushed. She looked towards Kevin. 'Don't you think that's sweet?'

'Took the words right out of my mouth,' said Kevin, fighting the urge to gag. 'Where is Ben, anyway?'

'Well, I asked him to come along, but he said he had homework to do,' Julie replied.

Kevin snorted, loudly. 'On a Saturday?'

'Brad? No. Not you, too!' sobbed a young woman's voice.

'Destroy the earthling female,' barked another voice – male, this time.

Ben lay back on his bed, his eyes glued to the sci-fi movie playing on his TV. He shovelled handfuls of popcorn into his mouth as he watched Brad, a blonde-haired highschool kid, begin shuffling towards his helpless girlfriend.

'Yes, master,' droned Brad, closing in on the girl. Ben shoved more popcorn into his mouth and chewed frantically. This was exciting stuff!

'No, Brad. Don't listen to him. You ... You love me!' cried the girl. 'Brad, nooooo!'

The picture froze, and a narrator's voice suddenly cut in. '*Brain Stealers from Outer Space* will be back, after this.'

As the movie went to an ad break, Ben reached for some more popcorn, only to find the bowl empty. He got up and headed for the kitchen to get a refill. He smiled as he poured more corn into the bowl. And to think, he could've missed this and gone shopping instead.

Across town, Kevin was still driving. He was trying to ignore the shopping talk going on in the back seat, but it was proving difficult to block out. He'd heard about so many sales and clothes store bargains that he almost wished a villain would appear and attack them, just so Gwen and Julie would change the subject.

Uh-oh.

A sudden movement in his rear view mirror caught Kevin's attention. Something was streaking towards the car. He couldn't quite make it out, but it seemed to be bright red, and was moving very, very fast.

BAD-OOOOM!

The road to the left of the car exploded in a shower of red sparks. Kevin yanked on the steering wheel, dodging right, just as another blast carved a hole in the tarmac behind them.

Kevin groaned below his breath. Why couldn't he just have been happy listening to the shopping talk?

CHAPTER TWO

SHIP SNATCHED

A third blast scorched through the air, striking the ground directly in front of Kevin's car. Frantically, Kevin threw the car into a skid, trying to avoid the damaged section of road. Smoke belched from the front tyres as they began to squeal loudly. With a sudden pop one of the tyres burst, and the car rumbled to a stop.

Overhead, Sir Morton of the Forever Knights swooped past on his flying Sky-Cycle, banking sharply as he swung round to take aim once again.

Gwen and Julie leapt from the back seat, taking cover behind the car. Kevin climbed from the front seat just as another laser blast hit the ground beside him, sending him sprawling on to the road.

'Why is he shooting at us?' asked Julie, her voice high and shrill.

'I don't know,' said Gwen, sighing. 'Everybody always shoots at us.'

With a wave of her hand, Gwen created an energy forcefield around them both, just as a series of blasts rained down on them from above.

'Watch the paint, that's four coats!' bellowed Kevin. He was back on his feet now, his eyes locked on the Forever Knight above him. Reaching out, he touched the roof of the car, changing his body into living metal.

Sir Morton took aim and unleashed another bolt of energy. It hit Kevin on the chest, staggering him backwards.

Meanwhile, Gwen had pulled out her mobile phone, and was hurriedly stabbing the buttons. She waited, impatiently, through four or five ringing tones, before a familiar voice finally answered.

'Hello?'

'Ben? Ellsworth Avenue, south of the mall. Now!'

Dropping the phone, Ben bounded off his

bed, sending the popcorn bowl tumbling on to the floor. With a twist of the dial and a slam of his hand, he activated the Omnitrix, and another incredible transformation took place.

'Jet Ray!' he cried, before throwing open his bedroom window and leaping out into the cool evening air.

Back at the car, Sir Morton had jumped down from his Sky-Cycle, and was doing this the old-fashioned way. His armoured fist slammed hard against Kevin's nose, forcing him backwards.

'Need help?' called Gwen.

'No, I'm good,' Kevin answered. He swung with a punch of his own, only to find it easily blocked by Sir Morton's shield. 'Nice Kinetic Phase shield,' said Kevin. 'What model is that, the Plestor 3?'

'Well, ain't you the observant one?' replied Sir Morton. The knight held an arm up above his head. At once, the energy lance from his Sky-Cycle flew to his hand. Taking aim, he unleashed a devastating laser blast at Kevin, driving him hard against the concrete ground.

'Kevin!' wailed Julie, taking a step towards her fallen friend.

'No, stay put, I'll handle this,' barked Gwen, pulling Julie back behind the car. Firing a few warning shots of magical energy, Gwen yelled, 'Back away from him!'

'Relax, girl,' sneered Sir Morton, turning to face her. 'It's not your boyfriend I'm after.'

With a flick of his wrist, the knight threw three silver disks towards the back of Kevin's car. They clamped on to the metal, and immediately began to emit a bright blue electrical light.

'Again with the car!' groaned Kevin, who was sick of seeing his beloved vehicle trashed over and over again.

The electricity crackled and cracked across the paintwork, and in moments a black and green blob fell from the back of the car and landed on the ground. It wailed and screeched as the electricity buzzed around it.

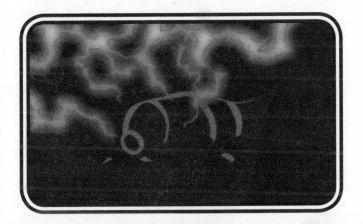

'Ship?' gasped Julie.

Gwen frowned, confused. 'Ship?'

Bending, Sir Morton scooped the squirming Ship up in a specially built container. 'In you go,' he said, clamping the top shut.

Without another word, the Forever Knight leapt aboard his Sky-Cycle, and rocketed off. As he raced through the air, he clipped the wing of a flying red alien, who was zooming in the opposite direction.

'Hey,' cried Jet Ray, when he had stopped tumbling through the sky. 'Someone needs a flying lesson, and I'm just the guy to . . .'

He spotted his friends down below, and decided to let the sky-hog go. Helping Gwen, Kevin and Julie was more important right now.

Touching down beside the others, Jet Ray transformed back into Ben. 'What happened?' he asked.

'That Flying Knight-in-a-Can fried my car,' Kevin moaned.

'And then he took my pet,' added Julie.

'Pet?' asked Ben.

'You know. Ship.'

'Ship?' gasped Ben. The last time he'd seen the little alien had been on his first date with Julie. He had no idea Julie had seen it again since then.

Ship was powerful – much more powerful than he looked. He didn't know why the Forever Knights would want him, but he knew it could only mean one thing.

Bad news.

A few minutes later, Ben and Julie were in the back of Kevin's car, while Kevin and Gwen sat up front. The damage to the road was holding traffic up, and they were now sitting in a slow-moving traffic jam.

'That guy is so paying for a new paint job,' Kevin seethed.

'Is that all you can think about?' asked Gwen, curtly. 'Your car?'

'No,' said Kevin, offended. 'Sometimes I think about food.'

'So,' began Ben, turning to Julie, 'how long has Ship been dropping by?'

'Every once in a while,' Julie shrugged. 'He comes, he goes, he shows me a new trick.'

'What kind of trick?'

'You know. Turning into things.'

'Why didn't you tell me?' Ben asked.

'You said you didn't want anything to do with Ship,' Julie reminded him.

'I never said that!'

Gwen turned in the front seat. 'Yes, you did.'

'OK, whatever,' Ben replied. 'But why would the Forever Knights want to steal Ship?'

'Please,' snorted Kevin, 'it can turn into anything it touches. It's like a Cup of Instant Weapon.'

'How fast can you get us home?' asked Ben.

Kevin wound down his window and leaned out. 'Hey, can you hurry it up?'

A few metres ahead of them, the driver of a tow truck leaned out of his own window and looked back. The towing arm of the truck was attached to the front of Kevin's car, and was pulling it slowly through the traffic.

'Sure,' said the driver, 'if you know how to fly!'

Kevin leaned back in his seat and slammed his hands against the steering wheel. The Forever Knights would pay for this, if it was the last thing he did!

Back at Kevin's garage, the car was already looking much better. It had taken a few hours, but Kevin had worked wonders.

'OK, new paint job and new tyres,' he said, proudly. He looked around, but the others were paying him no attention, so he returned to buffing up the paint.

Over by the door, Gwen was sitting on the floor. Her legs were crossed and her eyes were closed as she meditated. 'I'm searching for his manna,' she said, softly.

Ben raised an eyebrow. 'And?'

'And nothing,' Gwen confessed, opening

her eyes. 'Ship is technology, and I have trouble tracing stuff that isn't alive.'

'There's gotta be some way to find him,' said Ben.

'Didn't you say these Knights are, like, major English history geeks?' asked Julie. She held up an article in a newspaper she had been reading. 'It's a new housing development. Lancelot Lake Estates.'

Ben leaned closer and read the text. 'If a man's home is his castle, isn't it time you owned one?'

Gwen nodded. 'Possible.'

'Kind of a long shot,' Ben pointed out.

Julie folded the newspaper and stood up. 'I think we should check it out.'

'No, we will check it out,' said Ben, pointing to himself, Kevin and Gwen. 'You will stay here.'

'Ship's my pet, I want to help, you can't stop me,' said Julie, matter-of-factly. She brushed past Ben and got into the back of Kevin's car. A moment later, Kevin and Gwen climbed into the front seats.

'Great, guys,' sighed Ben, 'thanks for the support.'

CHAPTER THREE

ATTACK THE CASTLE

In the underground lab of the Forever Knights, a small round forcefield floated two metres above the ground. Inside the ball of energy, Ship bounced around frantically, hurling itself against the curved walls of the prison as it tried to find a way out.

'Scrappy little bloke, isn't he?' remarked Sir Morton, who was standing by Chadwick at the controls of a vast, complex-looking machine.

'Yes. But not so terribly bright.'

At the flick of a switch, the forcefield began to shrink. Ship screeched in panic as the glowing walls closed in around it, pinning its wriggling body in place.

Chadwick's fingers danced across the controls, and a large probe extended down through the energy field. Ship squealed as a small microchip was attached to the back of its head, then the little alien fell silent.

'Now,' smirked Chadwick, picking up a remote control, 'you will do as I command!'

With a press of a button on the controller, Ship's body went rigid. For a moment nothing else seemed to happen, but then the green areas of the alien's skin turned a deep, dark shade of red.

Kevin's car cruised along the street, looking better than ever. In the back seat, Julie had her arms folded, and was doing everything she could to avoid meeting Ben's eye.

'And we're not talking because . . .?' asked Ben.

'Because I am upset with you for being upset with me about Ship,' said Julie, curtly.

'Julie, we aren't talking about a poodle from the local pound,' said Ben, as softly as he could manage. 'You don't know what you're dealing with.'

'Yes I do,' Julie sniffed. 'I'm dealing with a person who was incredibly mean to poor little Ship, and who obviously doesn't trust me.'

'This isn't about trust, it's . . .' Ben stopped talking as he realised Gwen and Kevin were listening in to every word of the argument. He leaned in to Julie and whispered, 'You mind if we talk about this later?'

It wasn't difficult to find Lancelot Lakes. The entire estate was laid out like a medieval town, with each house built to look like a small castle, complete with towers and drawbridges.

Ben led the others through a clump of trees, and up to the side of a large mansion. He rapped his knuckles gently against the wall, only to discover what he thought was made of stone was actually made of metal, with the stone effect painted on.

'Looks like a giant miniature golf course,' he whispered.

'Is it time to bust the door down yet?' asked Kevin.

Ben edged open a side door. Peeking through the gap, he discovered that the door opened on to a small kitchen area. 'How about we try a more subtle approach for a change?'

Quietly, they all crept into the kitchen, easing the door closed behind them. There wasn't much to see, but another door led out into another part of the house. Tiptoeing quietly, Ben crossed to the door and opened it just a crack.

POP!

A sudden sound from behind him almost made Ben scream. He turned to find Kevin standing by the fridge, glugging down the contents of a can of fizzy cola.

'What?' asked Kevin, wiping his mouth with the back of his arm. 'I was thirsty!'

Ben gestured for Kevin to join him by the door, and all four of the heroes looked out through the gap.

'Whoa!' muttered Kevin, as his gaze fell on the dozen or more knights standing in the corridor beyond the door.

Ben's hand hovered above the Omnitrix, preparing to fight. Something made him hesitate, though. There was something about the way the knights were standing. Something . . . different.

Pushing open the door, he walked out into the corridor. None of the knights moved. Crossing to the closest one, he clicked his fingers in front of its visor. No response. They weren't knights at all, they were nothing more than decorative suits of armour.

Relaxing, Ben took hold of a curtain hanging behind the armour and held it up for the others to see. 'Do these drapes really go with chain mail?' he joked.

'Well, it works for us,' growled a deep voice.

Ben and the others spun to find Sir Morton standing behind them, blocking the doorway. Suddenly, the suits of armour lurched into life, each one raising a high-tech alien weapon and taking aim. Ben cursed below his breath. They'd walked right into a trap!

Leaping sideways, Ben barely avoided a stinging electrical blast from the knights' weapons. He hit the ground hard and rolled clumsily, landing behind an expensive-looking couch.

Another bolt screamed through the air towards Gwen. Raising her hands she tried to throw up a shield, but the force of the blast was too much. It shattered the shield and sent her tumbling backwards over the couch next to Ben.

'Are you OK?' he asked.

Gwen gritted her teeth. 'Better than them,' she growled, leaping to her feet and unleashing a wide stream of crackling energy. The beam hit Sir Morton on the backside and flipped him high into the air.

He landed on his back and found Kevin waiting for him. Yanking up the knight's visor, Kevin delivered a knock-out punch to his jaw, then quickly absorbed the metal of Morton's armour and launched an attack on another of the Forever Knights.

Another blast from Gwen knocked one of the villains' energy weapons from his hands. It tumbled through the air, its sharp metal edge soaring directly towards Julie's head.

'Look out!' Ben cried, clambering over the couch.

Twisting, Julie caught hold of the weapon's handle, and gripped it like a baseball bat.

'I meant duck, not –' Ben told her, before a metal-gloved fist caught him with a punch to the chin.

Another of the knights lunged for Julie, but she moved faster. Swinging the stolen weapon, she clattered it against the side of the knight's head. Even the armour couldn't save him, and he dropped to his knees, dazed.

'You're good at that,' smiled Gwen.

Julie flicked the weapon up and down a few times, each time clanging it against the stunned knight's head. 'It's a lot like tennis, actually,' she grinned.

Further along the corridor, Ben rolled behind another couch. He turned the control dial on the Omnitrix, but a searing energy blast tore through the fabric of the chair behind him, forcing him to roll to safety.

'Aw, c'mon already,' he complained, running for cover.

Kevin drove a metal knee into another

knight's stomach, putting an enormous dent in the villain's armour. 'Gwen,' Kevin cried, 'You wanna wrap this up?'

Wiping the sweat from her brow, Gwen nodded. Sweeping her arms up into the air, Gwen catapulted all the knights off the floor. They clattered together, then slammed hard against the side wall of the corridor.

A large section of the wall gave way, revealing a long staircase leading underground. Ben and the others watched as Sir Morton and the other knights tumbled and clanked down every single step.

'You know,' said Ben, leading the way down the stairs and past the unconscious knights, 'most accidents do happen in the home.'

'Oh, you young people are so amusing,' sneered a voice from the shadows.

Ben turned to see a scientist emerge from the gloom. A deep scar ran down his face, from the top to the bottom. In his hand he clutched a large remote control. 'And you would be?' asked Ben.

'Doctor Joseph Chadwick, director of technology for the Forever Knights. And you are the meddler who freed our ancient enemy, the Dragon.'

'I wouldn't say meddler,' Ben replied.

'Where's Ship?' demanded Julie.

'Ship?' spat Chadwick. 'Oh, is this what you mean?'

Chadwick punched a control on his pad and a red glow lit up the lab. His space craft rose silently into the air, its surface pulsing as if alive. Slowly, the craft turned and trained all its weapons on Ben and the others, as, behind them, Sir Morton and the knights got back to their feet.

Ben gulped. This, he thought, is not good.

CHAPTER FOUR

BIG TROUBLE!

Kevin's eyes went wide with horror as he spotted the largest of the flying craft's guns. 'Looks like an Antarian Obliterator,' he whispered. 'Nasty piece of work.'

'How nasty?' asked Ben.

'Fire!' bellowed Chadwick, and the gun unleashed a searing stream of proton energy. Julie, Gwen, Kevin and Ben scattered, narrowly avoiding the blast. Behind them, half of the basement wall exploded.

'Stay-outta-the-way nasty,' said Kevin. He took a look at the other weapons mounted on the ship. 'Galvan disruptor pods. Arcturian Plasers. Cassiopaean mass drivers. That thing's a flying arsenal.'

'Fire! Fire! Fire!' screamed Chadwick, gesturing wildly towards the heroes.

Ship didn't hesitate. Every one of its guns locked on and began firing. Ben pulled Julie behind a heavy stack of scientific equipment, as Kevin and Gwen took off in the opposite direction.

A stream of red flame scorched past Kevin's head, forcing him to drop to the ground. Pressing his hands against the concrete, he took on its strength, turning his body into living stone.

Before Kevin could get back up, a red targeting dot appeared on his chest. Ship was locking on, getting ready to fire once more!

'Get behind me!' yelled Gwen, stepping
up and raising a shield in front of them, just
as Ship unleashed more firepower. Gwen
staggered backwards, barely able to hold the
shield in place beneath the force of the energy
blasts.

She screamed as the shield finally gave
way, and then she sunk down on to the floor,
unconscious.

'Gwen!' cried Kevin, racing to help her.

'OK,' growled Ben, standing up and
activating the Omnitrix. 'Now I'm angry!'

In a blur of green energy, Ben transformed into the alien form he called Swampfire. Chadwick stepped back, surprised by this turn of events.

'Shoot it, shoot it, shoot it!' cried Kevin, pointing up at the floating Ship.

'No, Ben, no!' Julie yelped.

'Now, Ben, now!' Kevin urged.

Swampfire hesitated. He had a clear shot at Ship, but should he take it? Julie would never forgive him if he did, but maybe it was the only way they would survive. Or maybe, just maybe, there was another way.

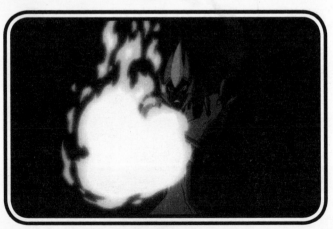

Holding his palms together, the alien hero formed a glowing ball of flame. Throwing his arms out he created a towering wall of fire around them, separating them from Chadwick, Ship and the Forever Knights.

'What was that?' sneered Kevin, hoisting Gwen up on to his shoulder.

Swampfire glanced down at Julie. She smiled up at him, gratefully. 'A compromise.'

Beyond the wall of flame, Chadwick was barking orders. 'Well, what are you waiting for?' he bellowed. 'Go!'

A wide nozzle extended from the underside of the floating space craft and took aim at the wall of flames. A burst of thick, white foam sprayed from the nozzle, smothering the fire in an instant.

Silently, the craft glided forwards. Swampfire and the others looked down to find targeting dots on their chests. Ship had them in his sights.

'We're toast,' Swampfire said.

'Indeed you are.' Chadwick stepped through the foam. His mouth was twisted into a smug grin. 'I have complete control over the creature. My wish is its command.'

'This is like that movie I was watching,' Swampfire realised. 'Brain Stealers from –'

'I thought you were doing homework?' snapped Julie.

Kevin shook his head.

'Can we discuss this later?' asked Swampfire, sheepishly. He tensed his muscles and studied the situation. Ship had its weapons locked on to them. Sir Morton and the Forever Knights had their weapons locked on to them. It didn't look good, but there had to be a way out of this. Maybe if he –

'Ship, stop. It's me, Julie.'

Swampfire gasped as Julie pushed past him, putting herself directly in Ship's line of fire.

'Ship, please,' she begged. 'Remember what you were. Are. Not a monster. Not a killer.' She smiled, warmly. 'You're a good boy, Ship. And you don't have to do what he says.'

Ship didn't respond. The red targeting dot glowed brightly on Julie's chest.

Chadwick stepped back, out of harm's way. 'I command you to fire all weapons at the intruders,' he ordered, turning his scarred face towards Ship. 'Now!'

Ship hung in the air, all its weapons trained on Julie, Kevin, Gwen and Ben. The control chip burned, flooding Ship's shape-shifting body with millions of electrical impulses.

Ship knew what it had to do. Its master had spoken. The orders were to destroy the human children, to wipe them off the face of the earth. The master had spoken, and the master must be obeyed.

But something about the girl made Ship hesitate. Deep inside the alien's mind, memories of Julie's kindness flickered. The girl wasn't Ship's enemy, she was Ship's friend.

KRRRRRRZZZZT!

A burst of green energy buzzed across the surface of the space craft, zapping the control chip and melting it into a metallic goo. The red glow that had covered Ship faded, revealing his true, green pattern beneath.

'How did you know that would work?' asked Swampfire, stunned.

Julie smirked. 'You're not the only one who's seen *Brain Stealers from Outer Space*.'

The huge war vessel began to collapse in on itself, growing smaller and smaller until only a friendly little blob with a wagging tail remained. Ship scampered over to Julie, and rubbed its head against the side of Julie's leg.

'Ship! Ship!' it chirped, happily.

Swampfire turned to Kevin. '"Shoot it, shoot it, shoot it!"' he said, mimicking Kevin's voice.

Kevin shrugged, but looked a little guilty. 'It was a suggestion.'

'A suggestion we'll be happy to take,' growled Chadwick. Around him, Sir Morton and the other Forever Knights got into position and took aim with their weapons. More knights raced to take up positions around the heroes, until they were surrounded on all sides. Ship might be back on the side of good, but the battle wasn't over yet.

CHAPTER FIVE

THE BATTLE TURNS

In a flash, Ship hurled itself into the air, transforming as it moved. It took less than a second for the friendly blob to transform back into the flying war machine. This time, though, its weapons were trained squarely on Chadwick and the knights.

'Uh-oh,' said Swampfire, trying not to laugh.

Chadwick swallowed nervously. 'Sir Morton?' he said, glancing across to the knight. 'Would you kindly ask your men to lower their weapons? Please?'

Sir Morton clicked his visor down over his face. 'Sorry, Doc,' he answered. 'It's time we got rid of this bunch, even if we all gotta go in the bargain.'

Raising his weapon, Morton fired a stinging energy blast at Ship. The other knights followed their commander's lead, and soon bright arcs of energy were snaking from the basement on all sides, rocking Ship in mid-air.

Priming its own weapons, Ship returned fire. Huge chunks of stone, and broken lab equipment were tossed into the air as Ship rained down blast after blast on the attacking knights.

Alerted by the sounds of battle, more knights flooded in from the mansion above. Rather than attack Ship, however, these newcomers targeted Swampfire, Kevin and the girls.

Gwen's shield deflected a few power beams, but the knights were closing in all around.

'Not liking where this is going,' Kevin groaned, realising they were vastly outnumbered.

The Forever Knights' blasts, and the high-pitched screams of Ship's own weapons were making it impossible to hear anyone approaching. That was why Swampfire didn't notice the knight sneaking up on him until it was too late.

A surge of electrical energy sliced through the alien hero's left arm, cutting it clean off. Swampfire roared with pain, but the damage wasn't all that bad. As the shocked knight watched on, a new arm grew from the stump of Swampfire's old one.

When the arm had fully grown back, Swampfire clenched his new hand into a fist, and punched the Forever Knight all the way to the other side of the basement.

Chadwick cowered behind Sir Morton, tears stinging his eyes. He was a coward – he was happy being a coward – and he would have loved to run away and hide. But there was nowhere for him to run to, the battle was blocking the exit. All he could do was duck down behind Sir Morton, and hope the knight's armoured body was big enough to protect them both.

Sir Morton roared with rage and pumped a few blasts towards Ship. The craft spun and aimed all its weapons at the Forever Knight commander. Chadwick whimpered, threw his hands over his head, and ran for safety, just as Ship opened fire. Morton howled as he was sent crashing against the back wall of the basement, before he landed in a crumpled heap on the floor.

Still the battle raged on. The knights were closing in on Swampfire and the others, firing bolt after bolt in their direction. Gwen did her best to shield them from the worst of the blasts, but there were too many of them, and she knew she couldn't keep it up much longer.

With a faint whine of its engines, Ship descended until it was just half a metre above the ground, and lowered its entrance ramp. Swampfire grabbed Julie and led her up the ramp, with Kevin and Gwen racing up behind them.

At the top of the ramp, Swampfire stopped. A row of knights hurried towards them, weapons raised and ready to fire. With a thrust of his arm, he sent a fireball spiralling towards them.

Incredibly, every one of the knights managed to leap out of the way. They rolled on the floor, then got back up, guns primed. They almost congratulated themselves on how easily they'd evaded the fireball, before they realised it hadn't been aimed at them.

Behind them, a wide, gaping hole had

been burned through one of the lab's gas tanks. They turned back to Ship, to see the entrance ramp sliding closed. The last thing they saw before it slammed shut was the smirking face of Swampfire.

BAD-OOOOM!

A massive explosion ripped through the underground lair, tearing apart all Chadwick's lab equipment. Huge chunks of masonry fell from the roof, smashing into the floor and showering the knights with dust and rubble.

Sir Morton heaved himself back to his feet. He looked around and realised at once that the battle was lost. 'Run away, run away!' he cried, clanking noisily towards the ruined remains of the stairs.

Tears streamed down Chadwick's face as he scurried around in a circle, too panicked to find the way out. His plan was ruined. His lab was ruined. Any minute now he could be squashed by a lump of falling rock. This really wasn't turning out to be his day!

As the explosion rocked the rest of the house, Ship rose higher into the air. Its engines gave a loud whirr as it lurched sharply upwards, breaking through the roof of the house just as the walls began to collapse.

Angling itself upwards, Ship took off at tremendous speed, streaking high into the sky. Clouds shot past so fast they were little more than a blur. Now back in human form, Ben gripped on to his seat so hard his knuckles turned white.

'G-good ship,' he stammered. 'Down boy!'

But Ship wasn't listening. It banked sharply, almost throwing the four passengers out of their seats. Rising at a steep angle for a few hundred metres, it suddenly turned and plunged downwards, racing towards the town below at maximum thrust.

Up front, Ben and Kevin exchanged a worried look. There were no controls inside the craft, so all they could do was stare out through the windscreen and hope not to crash.

Behind them, even Gwen was getting nervous. She was gripping her own chair tightly, when a sound to her left made her turn. Julie was relaxing in her seat, giggling so hard she could barely breathe. She knew Ship better than the others, and knew that, like all pets, Ship loved to play.

With a roar of air brakes, Ship came to an abrupt stop less than a metre above Julie's garden. The imprint of the submarine was still there, as were the broken fence and uprooted tree.

The heroes noticed none of these things, as Ship opened the entrance hatch and let them spill out on to the grass.

'Cool,' said Kevin, who was the first to get back to his feet. He looked admiringly at Ship. 'We have our own spaceship.'

'I have my own spaceship,' corrected Julie. Beside her, Ship transformed back into blob mode and leapt up into her arms.

'But we can borrow it sometimes, right?' asked Ben, eagerly.

Gwen sighed. 'Why do we even need a spaceship?'

Kevin thought for a moment, but came up blank. 'Well, you know,' he said, 'for space stuff.'

'You can borrow him if you help me take care of him,' said Julie, smiling. 'Walking him, playing with him.'

Ben nodded. 'OK, Ship,' he said, 'find me a ball and we can play catch.'

Excitedly, Ship launched itself into the air. Ben watched in horror as it transformed its putty-like body into the shape of an enormous baseball. A large round shadow passed across Ben as Ship came plummeting towards him.

'Ow!' Ben yelped, as the enormous ball hammered him down on to the grass. On reflection, he thought, maybe having a spaceship would be far more trouble than it was worth!